I0539776

FAILED ANGELS

Francesco Pagot

www.theperfectedition.com

First published in United Kingdom
by The Perfect Edition in 2012

copyright © 2012 Francesco Pagot

The moral right of the author has been asserted.

*All characters and events in this publication other than those
clearly in the public domain are fictitious and any resemblance to
real persons living or dead is purely coincidental.*

All rights reserved.
No part of this publication may be reproduced, stored in a
retrieval system or transmitted in any form or by any
means without the prior permission in writing of the pub-
lisher not to be otherwise circulated in any form of bind-
ing or cover other than that in which it is published and
without similar conditions including this condition being
imposed on the subsequent purchaser.
Photos and illustrations by Francesco Pagot

A CIP catalogue record for this book is available
from the British library
US Library of Congress registration Number
has been applied for
ISBN code: 978-0-9568180-8-9

The Perfect Edition
Communications House 26 York Street
London W1U 6PZ United Kingdom

info@theperfectedition.com
www.theperfectedition.com

To my Guardian Angel,
because no Angel has ever been busier.

By the same author:
BEDDA MATRI (THE BEAUTIFUL MOTHER)
ONLY TIME WILL TELL
GREENHORN

CONTENTS

ACKNOWLEDGMENTS

I was very tempted to skip the Acknowledgement page all together, because surely I am going to leave somebody off who thinks they deserve to be on here.

I probably should be sending instead a nice thank you note and maybe some chocolate to those who really helped with the book especially my editor, Lisa Cole, she is truly overworked and underpaid and she makes my books better.

But for sure I don't want to miss thanking the wonderful people and film crew members in Mumbai, of which there are too many to list here.

A big hug to Keiko Nagai, always so helpful and supportive.

I am truly thankful to Dave Judge who always says it as it is, only a true friend does that.

Thank you also to Sue and Terry Bamber for the constant encouragement and kindness.

A special thank you to Richard Bedser, his words of wisdom never fail to guide me.

To my family, Cristina, Enrico and Elena, true angels of my life.

Failure teaches success.

(Japanese saying)

PREFACE

I have to thank an angel in Mumbai for this book, a little Cupid on the Mumbai Film Studios stage 4 door.

I was recently working there and I spotted that little winged creature high up.

The little rascal was drawing his bow to lose the arrow that creates so much damage amongst lovers, waking up hearts.

The idea to publish these short screenplays came to me there and then, like a capricious arrow out of the blue that woke me up.

These stories, short and bittersweet, have been sleeping in the virtual drawers of my laptop for a while, a long while, it was time to let them out.

This small collection of short narrations deserves a little self-indulgent book.

There is a saying in the film industry, "short stories have short legs" and it is a long-standing phrase that is ever so true. Contrary to common perception very few actors or directors owe their success to a short film, most of these pieces are destined to enter oblivion and I hope nobody will mind if I say "quite rightly so" in most cases.

It is difficult enough to write a short story, let alone write about how to write one.

If they truly work as a short narration, ideally with a twist at the end of the tale, some overly excited readers often say 'have you ever thought about turning this into a feature length film?'

The answer often is "yes, I did think about it, but it would never work". Short stories only work if they are kept short, rarely otherwise.

One of the reasons why people like them is because they are short, as in 'limited in time'.

On the other hand, they are normally short-lived because they are unfortunately short, and because of that difficult to market commercially.

When it comes to writing for the screen there is one big factor to consider: exposure.

Most of the time short films find success only within a limited audience, normally made of self-congratulating filmmakers.

I know many excellent directors who have made

some brilliant, actually let me rephrase that, some extremely brilliant and award-winning shorts, nevertheless they are still struggling to get the necessary recognition they so truly deserve.

Why? The answer is shortly brutal, shorts have short legs, they don't walk far carrying your talent.

There is a general perception that some now well known directors have made their name at the start of their career producing a short story, grabbing some movie mogul's attention and purse.

Even if that was true nowadays there are no more producers or movie moguls with that vision.

To see the potential talent that someone has, just looking at a short film, requires a particular acumen that today's majority of movie execs lacks.

There was a time when directors who came from the world of commercials, (I mean TV adverts, the 30 seconds little stories), enjoyed success on the strength of that alone.

Adrian Lyne, Ridley and Tony Scott and many more came from the ephemeral world of advertising, shooting stories that could only span a few precious seconds but needed to convey so much in so little time that marked them out as geniuses overnight.

These directors became famed and respected filmmakers spanning their talents over many seconds on screen, eventually stretching their skills over the 90 minutes length of a movie in the cinema.

Someone like David Lynch started his career producing his own little quirky and dark short films that eventually became the trademark style of his movie career.

In the past the short film was almost a necessary passage to demonstrate your vision and talent; Tim Burton made some fab shorts to kick-start his director's production and so did Steven Spielberg. The aforementioned are all incredible talents, but the brilliance of their short films wasn't the reason for their late fame.

Nowadays short films are seen as desperate attempts to grab attention, and indeed they are such a thing, but there are so many bad ones that the good ones disappear into the magma of badly produced, horrendously boring and pathetically arty short productions clogging film festivals.

Sitting as a juror one often wonders why everyone writes the same short story involving identity crisis, vacuum cleaners (you read correctly) and the same character who questions his daily life and looks for more.

The only use for a screenplay is to be made into a film, this is even truer if that screenplay is shorter that the standard 120 pages of a 90 minute movie.

These short scripts were conceived many years ago

to help directors' careers or to bring attention to a particular subject, but fate, that capricious wind driven arrow, decided otherwise.

Some of these stories have received awards or peer recognition, however they haven't felt the love of a broader audience.

Short stories are like mayflies, these tiny winged aquatic insects whose lifespan as adults can vary from just 30 minutes to one day depending on the species. The primary function of the adult mayfly is reproduction; a short screenplay has a similar purpose seeking to give birth to the story onto a screen, even if it lasts only 15 minutes.

It is now up to you to decide if it was worth reading them, but please be lenient, after all they take up very little of your time.

Like a mayfly that has gone off its course and failed, these shorts are little winged angels that the wind of fate decided to stop in their mission.

I like to think that like angels they did their best to impress and conquer, but unfortunately they did not succeed. Everyone deserves a second chance, even if it's short lived.

1. WET THE BABY'S HEAD

This is a fifteen minutes short that I wrote back in 1990. The story came to me after reading about a baby who was washed away by a freak wave while playing on a beach with his parents. A peaceful and sunny day, a totally calm and placid sea and suddenly the baby was gone. Forever.

The screenplay was selected by Granada television in a competition, but at the last minute they changed their mind and went on to produce something else. I have altered it very little from the original, just something here and there to make reading a bit easier. Often I edited out much of the jargon that screenplays have, such as camera or editing technicalities that can be quite distracting if one is not used to them. I have only kept a mention of the camera angle when it helps to convey the point of view in relation to the scene; after

11

all you write a screenplay thinking of an audience, as you write a book thinking of a reader.

For the narrating voice I always thought of Stephen Fry, I love the warmth and quirkiness of intonation that this amazing thespian can produce.

The following is what I wrote at the time to accompany the script, it still stands true.

Shock and horror are what our narrating voice describes to us: from a calm, reassuring environment to one of loud cacophony, invasive curiosity. This is reflected in the photography with stark, raw images, fast camera movements, distorted faces. At first everything should be overwhelming, loud, crass and crude. Our narrator who has quite a quirky voice, makes us realise what a silly way of living this is. Slowly acclimatising to this new world the camera movements become more composed, but we should still keep the sound and voices distorted and much too loud. Only in the presence of the sea do we feel calm and relaxed. Except for the baby's mother the other characters are grotesque and unpleasant, not evil, just not people you would like to share a boat with for long days at sea. At times eerie music accompanies the story, it has a water like quality to its notes. The creatures at the end are semi-transparent, like plankton. For some scenes (salmon jumping, turtles crawling) stock footage is an option. It's a dark and magical comedy told from the perspective of someone who didn't ask to come into

12

this world, but like all of us, didn't have much choice.

I always had a strange affection for this script, maybe because I love water so much.

Fade in from black screen.

The screen is filled by calm deep blue water.

Muffled sounds are heard off screen, it feels as if we're inside a water tank.

A feeble light appears in the distance.

Suddenly the water starts rushing towards the light, now more intense.

Dragged by the current as if on a rollercoaster we are rushing towards what now looks like an opening.

The sequence becomes our point of view as we land on a midwife's lap, littered with blood and the messy stuff that a new born brings with him coming into this world.

A male voice over is heard off-screen, talking warmly. It will stay with us throughout, as if we can hear someone's thoughts, the baby's thoughts.

"I knew I was born because the water turned into blood."

We find ourselves inside a hospital's labour room.

We can make out indistinct silhouettes of people

looking into the audience. Loud comments and noises are reverberating unpleasantly; it feels like a serious hangover on a Sunday morning.

The male voice over is talking as if they are in slight pain: "I felt so unsafe, vulnerable and heavy."

In the same room we witness a young nurse weighing the baby.

She shakes her head, obviously finding him far too small too small and underweight.

Cut to a overhead view of the baby on the scales, struggling to get up. The male voice over resumes with a sigh, "I was fished into this world and now I'm stuck."

We now see the baby's point of view as people titillate him and make faces with grotesque effect. Last appearing into frame is a woman in her late 40s, heavily made up, sporting enough jewellery to sink a pirate's ship.

She's examining the baby like an entomologist who has found a new specimen.

The woman speaks loudly and disdainfully: "Is he normal?"

The tired expression of the baby's mother is the silent answer.

The camera moves onto the woman who just spoke, Aunt Claire's inquisitive face now is filling the screen in all her bad hair days glory.

Once again the male voice over clarifies for the audience: "Meet Aunt Claire, mum's sister. Auntie now sponges off us since father died."

Aunt Claire speaks again, even louder:

"He's a bit... weird."

The narrating voice is quick to retaliate:

"She's the freak: half woman half implant. Me, well…"

We now see a big close up of the baby's face; he's quite weird indeed, with strange pointy ears, big bulging eyes. The male voice over carries on sweetly:

"…a face only mum can love."

We observe the same room as a wider scene, time has passed and the mother lies in bed, gazing at the falling snow visible outside the window. The baby is resting on her chest.

Some doctors and consultants are busy discussing amongst each other, standing around the baby's mother. The atmosphere is so thick that even a surgeon's scalpel couldn't slice it.

The male voice over is commenting quietly:

"I couldn't understand that word they used, something to do with my lungs, a rare malfunction."

The muttering of the doctors becomes audible, words like sea, iodine and similar are echoing.

Two nurses walk by, chatting amongst themselves.

We just hear glimpses of their conversation, as one nurse says: '- found her near the shipwreck." And the other mutters: "- husband drowned."

A different moment, much later, we are still in a hospital room, the mother is asleep, the baby resting on top of her.

We now see the exterior of a house on a beach, it is late afternoon.

Several months have gone by and the baby and his mother are both sitting on the beach, facing the sea. Next to her is a bowl with a goldfish and all three of them (fish included) are looking at the waves caressing the beach.

As we observe the calm sea grey against a grey sky we hear the voice resonating off screen.

"The sea looks so tired, the winter is nearly over. Sand, sea and sky, all blends together as if reluctant to be separated by the strong colours of the summer to come."

Suddenly we hear a loud yell coming from the house.

Auntie Claire is announcing dinner and Colin, her husband stands next to her.

The voice reprises narration: "Meet Colin, now his waistline is more like a coastline."

We can see that Colin is very fat indeed.

Inside the beach house we can see the kitchen, it is now morning and Colin is having a whale of a breakfast.

He's also blowing into an inflatable armband at the same time; frosties, jam and fluids oozing onto his chin, not a pretty sight.

The baby's mother is sitting on an armchair breast-feeding.

While the baby is sucking avidly we move closer onto his face.

The usual accompanying voice is now almost pensive: "I always wonder: if I blow into this one, does the other one get bigger?

Suddenly, with a loud 'ta-daa!' Auntie Claire enters the scene, next to Colin.

She's wearing only a bikini, if one can call it that.

Colin freezes, spoonful of frosties suspended in mid air.

The fully inflated armband attached to his lips slowly deflates, emitting a noise that's a perfect raspberry. Colin's reaction is truly aghast: "What's that?"

Auntie Claire's is jolly and quick: "A bikini!"

"That's more like a nicotinette patch with a string." Colin's answer provokes a shouting contest as mother and baby leave the room.

The beach is calm and the mother is resting on a long chair while the baby is playing on the sand, she's half asleep. Baby is exploring the surroundings. Suddenly he aims decisively towards the sea.

The narrator's voice accompanies his movements: "Don't do this, don't do that, go with the flow. But what if the right direction of the flow is the one indicated by salmon?"

A series of rapidly cut scenes follow.

A overhead view of the baby as he speeds on all fours is followed by a similar top view of a baby turtle crawling on sand towards the sea.

Baby and turtle look incredibly similar during their attempt.

Suddenly the turtle is snatched by a frigate bird, and similarly baby is suddenly snatched by Aunt Claire, inches from the enticing water.

As the baby flies in Auntie's arms we can hear the voice with his usual aplomb: "No point struggling, it would be like attempting synchronized swimming in a force ten gale."

We see Auntie Claire carrying the baby back into the house, shouting abusively at her sister who just stares blankly from her chair at the sea, mesmerised.

The scene changes to a frigate bird flying away with its young prey, the baby turtle.

The sun sets and in the evening darkness we can make out gently flowing waves, undulating silk under the stars.

Inside the beach house everyone is in the dining room.

Colin, oblivious to the others, resembling a sea lion marking his territory, greedily grabs some seafood.

Auntie Claire is sipping a foul looking slim fast instant milkshake through a straw.

Her loud slurping indicates she's quite orgasmic about it.

Nearby the baby's mother is lost in her thoughts, as lost as are the veggies on her plate.

She slowly turns her head towards the baby in a highchair, also ignoring the nearly empty bowl of milk in front of them, fixating on Colin's voracity.

From the baby's point of view we can also observe Colin stuffing himself, perplexed at the misery of his companions. The big man suddenly opens his mouth brimming with food.

"C'mon, it's all water under the bridge, let's get on with life and be merry!"

He then burps loudly, as he raises a can of lager towards the baby.

"Let's wet the baby's head!"

He takes a large gulp from the can and impervious to the others picks up a sardine from his plate. With a well-practiced gesture he tosses the poor fish into the air and catches it in his mouth.

Then with a clownish smile he turns to the baby sitting to his right, leaning towards him, slowly making the sardine reappear through his lips, teasing the baby.

We see the baby's horrified expression, staring at the poor sardine between Colin's lips.

Then all of a sudden: "Phoaar!"

Colin's face receives the full geyser blast of regurgitated milk propelled by the baby.

Everyone screams, everyone except the baby's mother.

Later on in the baby's room we can only hear the sound of waves in the distance. As we look around the room we come across the baby trying to climb out of the cot.

The narrating voice is soothing but slightly annoyed.

"So who came up with this gravity thing?"

We see the baby falling on his back after losing his grip.

"Ok, it keeps houses and big pieces of furniture from flying around and hurting people."

We witness another attempt to climb over the edge ending up with the baby legs up in the air at the bottom of the cot.

At the same time we see a quick scene of a salmon's vain effort to swim up current, jumping over rocks.

As we get back to the bedroom we can see the baby is trying again undefeated.

"Ok, gravity keeps planets aligned too."

We can see the intense expression as he continues his attempts.

"Well, it may be a good force for the universe but it's an evil force for-"

Whack! He falls onto his back inside the cot again. With a whimper the voice continues: "-anyone who was once floating freely."

Relentlessly he tries again, this time successfully and we accompany the baby as he crawls through the house at speed.

Everything's quiet, like the sea. The sand shining with moonlight, firm in the chill of the night, is just perfect for the baby to cruise full steam ahead.

The voice is now quite excited. "The melting of snow this year will not have me as a witness."

Suddenly the baby stops. From the baby's face frozen with enchantment, we pull back to reveal a wave gently enveloping the baby with soft silvery froth. As the wave retreats we notice that the baby has disappeared into the blue sea.

We cut away to find the baby now swimming underwater, happily and effortlessly.

Once again we hear his thoughts: "A good fish tale always has a fresh twist."

As we move away we pull up and high, watching the sea murmuring beneath the stars.

A time lapse effect sees daylight brought by the sun rising revealing a policeman who is following tiny prints on the sand: the baby's route.

We fly away and find Auntie Claire, a blabbering mess: mascara running down her cheeks, her face looking like a chewed jellyfish.

Colin is not far away, appearing next to Aunt Claire, disbelief tattooed on his face.

He's sipping soup from a bowl with a little mermaid painted on.

At the sight of the bowl Aunt Claire erupts into hysterical sobbing, while Colin tries to hide baby's bowl from her view.

We move around and now see the baby's mother, composed with surreal calm, oblivious to the frenzy of policemen, paramedics and curious joggers.

In the distance Police rescue divers in full scuba gear are about to enter the water, their movements are closely observed by mother.

We move closer to her face, serene and strangely present for the first time.

A faded smile appears on her lips.

Auntie Claire's outcry is heard off screen: "insane" is what she is repeating obsessively.

On the screen a big close up of baby's serene face underwater, a smile appears on his lips, then a giggle, followed by a range of joyful expressions from someone who is in his true element: calm blue water. An indistinct silhouette approaches him from behind, a beautiful mermaid, tail gleaming of mother-of-pearl, playfully touching the baby's hands.

A second creature, baby's mirror image in years to come, appears from below joining in.

We can now fully observe the baby's ecstatic expression. The tone of his thoughts echoes more serene than ever before: "I knew I was home because the water was blue again."

Muffled sounds are audible, as if the outside world has been wrapped in a blanket, the word "insane" echoing distortedly in the distance.

"I knew I was safe once more."

The baby is now swimming away into the blue. He stops and suddenly turns towards the audience: "What did you say? I can't hear you."

The baby's words float away, like oil on water.

Fade to black, the end credits roll in.

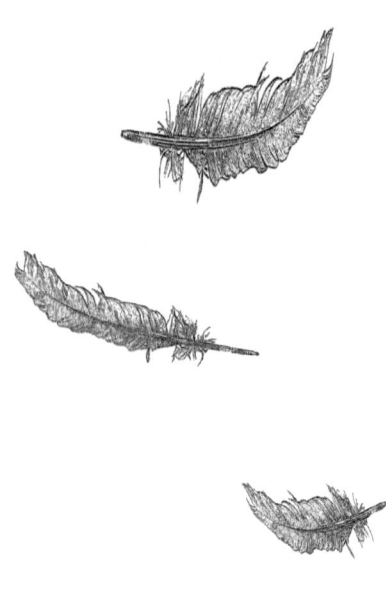

24

2. THE BEST OF LUCK

The idea for this came to me while I was out walking to buy some groceries. Just outside the supermarket there was this poor guy, a true mental case, shouting repeatedly 'the best of luck!' to everyone who was walking past. He was a real character and his desperate well wishing cry stayed with me for a while. Not long after that day I was asked by a director to write something in the Cohen brothers' style.

Luck has always played a big part in the brothers' plots and I remembered this catchphrase heard in the street and wrote something in which luck plays a big part. It was never produced because the director later on wanted something more Tarantinesque, more blood and gore, less luck.

Written in 2002 it has all the usual ingredients of double crossings, mind games and carefully laid out plans which are interfered with by a cruel fate.

The struggle of the protagonist is the eternal battle for survival, at any cost, whatever it takes.

The dialogue is full of swear words and gangster jargon, but that is the way the underworld talks, or in any case how most people perceive they talk.

What obviously characterises these types of scripts is violence, and even if there is some brutal action, the real threat comes from the underlining suggestion that something even more violent is about to happen at any moment. The narrative develops like an elastic band that keeps getting stretched and at one point it will snap, and someone will get hurt badly.

A forest's canopy of leaves is sprinkled with sunlight. The wind blows some leaves as a woman in her late twenties enters the frame.

She wears   heavily applied make-up; a tight evening frock shaping her thin figure. The high heels she is wearing make her look even more fragile and definitely out of place.

We also notice that someone wearing heavy boots is following closely.

He is wearing a black suit as black as his coat, a hat and sunglasses. He is lean and mean, moustache hiding lips not used to smiling.

The woman is clearly struggling on the rough terrain. She is shivering even if it doesn't seem to be a cold day.

The man is confidently following, hands deep in his pockets.

The woman suddenly trips and stumbles over. She picks up one of her shoes. The heel is missing.

The man speaks first, his voice has no emotions: "Get up Millie."

Millie is still on the ground, trembling.

"I can't, I can't-"

Thump! A sharp kick sends the shoe in the air.

"You're better off without it."

"I'm not in a hurry Leo, besides my ankle is broken."

Leo takes his right hand out of his pocket: a big gun fills his palm.

"You can drag your foot or I can drag you stiff; your choice."

"Why not carry me in your strong arms?"

Her voice becomes softer as she pulls herself closer to Leo.

She is almost purring: "I won't bite you."

A chilling smile flashes across Leo's face. He crouches next to her and puts the gun in his pocket. His hand reaches out to Millie's face, open palmed, with lightning speed.

Whack!

A vicious blow on her mouth with his open palm sends Millie flat on her back; blood makes the red lipstick more vivid.

"Red suits you, especially when your lips grow bigger."

Millie is now trying to get up. Tears black with mascara run down her cheeks. She stares after Leo with eyes like poison.

Leo is enjoying the show; he runs his finger onto her face, stopping black mascara tears.

"Who's the war paint for? I see. I suppose a blowjob's now out of the question."

Millie answer comes quickly under her breath: "I'd rather die."

"Funny you say that."

Leo drags Millie to her feet: "Is that your last wish?"

The sun is now glinting warmer, the odd sunray caressing Leo and Millie walking into the woods. The cover provided by the trees gives an effect of cathedral like darkness. The sun filters down through the leaves in gently shifting patterns.

Leo is whistling as Millie is walking and sobbing. She suddenly stops, leaning against a tree. Leo does the same leaning on the other side of the large tree trunk. He stops whistling.

Millie is looking around as if hoping some inspiration could appear from the towering trees.

She breathes deeply, very deeply. Her words come out in a fast faintly broken sequence.

"Don't do this to me Leo, please! You know I'm scared, I'm really scared, c'mon, you can't do this ...you know it wasn't me, I'll prove it... gimme a chance, let me go, I'm begging you. I'm not bad; I've never hurt anybody. I can keep my mouth shut nobody will know. I don't want to die... pleaaase Leo. I'm talking to your heart."

Leo is watching the sky, face drawn, silent. What heart?

Millie's shaking voice strains for a tone of reasonableness.

"I know what Nic has told you, but think about it. It doesn't make any sense. If I took the bloody money, why wait like a bunny staring at the lights of the oncoming car? You're making me too smart, but I'm the one who's getting squashed under the bumper. Honest to God I have no idea why Nic is doing this."

Millie moves away from the tree ending up facing Leo, who keeps staring ahead as if Millie's not there, now their faces are in profile.

She carries on, warming her tone a little: "Why is Nic doing this Leo? Is it some kind of game? Is it a test? He's testing me, isn't he? 'Twist her ear and watch her squeal' is that what he told you? Huh? Well you can spare yourself the sweat, there ain't any juice coming out of this lemon, never mind how hard you squeeze and twist! I didn't take the fuckin' money and you can tell that to Mr God almighty!"

Her voice echoes amongst the trees, followed by an eerie silence broken only by Millie's heavy breathing.

Leo looks into Millie's eyes; right through them like a surgeon does before extracting a foreign body, this is the truth in Millie's case.

"If I look deeper into all the shit that just came out of your mouth I will find a precious gem. Is that so?"

Millie waves her head affirmatively

Leo carries on. "I'll have to believe you, because it stinks really badly. But if what you're saying is right it means the word of God isn't the truth. Are you fuckin' religious Millie?"

Millie looks away nervously, incapable of finding an answer.

Leo's next words come out more like a hiss: "Back to earth: are you saying that Nic is lying?"

"No Leo, I'm not saying that, I mean, not exactly."

"It's useless to put on your breaks when you're up-side down. Now let me rephrase it for you: is Nic lying?"

Millie's tears are now filling her mouth.

"Fuck Nic! Nic is a sick fuck!"

Whack! With a well-practised movement Leo's hand connects with Millie's face once again.

"You know it well Leo, that's why you can't do me."

"What type of girl are you Millie? The dumb one? Nah. The girl next door? I doubt it. The tough broad type?"

"I'm the type of girl who doesn't like to be a type. That's why-"

Millie protects her face with both hands fearing another blow.

"-That's why Nic can't cope with my type. He only surrounds himself with people who lick his ass so deep he doesn't need to brush his teeth anymore."

A long silence follows. Millie is now checking Leo's reaction: nothing, wooden as the tree trunk next to him. Reassured Millie slowly lets her guard down and starts playing with her frock.

"It's not the money. Nic wraps fish with what's missing. He's getting paranoid; he doesn't trust anybody anymore he's a sick puppy."

Whack! The 'sick' word detonates another blow, this time sending Millie to the ground.

Millie's face hits the ground. Leo's hand enters the frame, grabbing Millie by the hair, and he ends up sitting on Millie's back, knees on the side, pinning her face down.

He puts his mouth right next to her ears, so she won't miss a word.

"That's quite a rough speech coming out of your sweet lips. What have you been up to recently, sanding back the bumps of buses with your tongue?"

Naturally Millie says nothing, touching her lips with the tip of her tongue, to ease the pain.

Leo takes a deep breath trying to control his anger.

"Nic sent me because he trusts me: is that too difficult for you to believe? Trust as in belief, loyalty, and faith. Fuckin' fidelity. Does that sound Greek to you? Do you want me to spell it out? Fuckin' bitch."

Leo gets up, panting; Millie stays down, a babbling mess.

"Get up and don't sell me the hooker with the heart of gold. And don't worry, I'll shut your mouth forever as soon as we are far enough from the road and that won't be soon enough, fuckin' forest!"

Millie slowly gets up, not a pretty sight anymore, yet she tries to wipe some of the dirt off her face.

She hesitates a little, then: "What if..."

She gets a grip on herself.

"What if I've really taken the money?"

That definitely got Leo's attention. He narrows his eyes as he removes his sunglasses.

Millie continues, almost fearless.

"If... only if."

"-If- is short for fuck-up. Don't play with me, you're talking money or you're talking shit and I don't like multiple choices."

Millie is now looking at Leo almost imploring.

"We can split; that would be better actually, just leave me enough to get out of the game."

Leo's answer comes out as dry as wood: "How cute: you can't face the drama anymore Mrs Shakespeare?"

Leo is on a roll.

"Is the play too gruesome or maybe you've guessed the ending? Was it me? Did I spoil everything? Or was it Nic who's spoilt you: Millie here, Millie there... the original Mrs Jesus?"

"Leo... Leo please listen to me: I used to like Nic but now he sniffs enough shit to insulate a loft, he's changed, you're the only one who still trusts him, but he doesn't trust you anymore."

Judging from Leo's expression she has touched the right nerve.

"Nic sent you to waste me not because he trusts you, but because you'll make things easier for him."

Leo can't resist this one.

"What are you blabbering about?"

A hint of a smile appears on Millie's face: gotcha!

"I've heard stuff."

"What do you mean you've heard stuff? Do you feel little men running around in your head?"

"Stuff... you know, smoke, rumours."

"What fuckin' rumours?"

Millie takes some time before saying anything; she doesn't want to waste the bait that will hook Leo for good.

"Smell the coffee Leo: who's the only badass who can take Nic's place?"

Millie observes him carefully.

"Hulk? Mother fuckin' Theresa?"

Silence. Only Millie's words are echoing in the woods

Leo wanders around in a circle, like a horse on a leash. Millie is holding tight.

"You'd say you have a cock under that frock to save your ass."

Millie is quick to answer: "Let's go back to the car: if I'm right we'll find company, if not..."

Leo is staring hard; Millie slumps a bit realising how thin her tactic is.

"If not, tough luck."

"Luck huh? Since when do you believe in luck?"

Millie shrugs; nothing much matters at this point.

"Luck sucks, but what have you got to lose, give it a shot, as a figure of speech... I mean."

"What about the money? Was that your shot?"

Millie slowly walks away from Leo, to avoid his inquisitive look

"If I say yes, you won't believe me, but you won't buy it even if I say no. If someone is waiting for you at the car it means I didn't do it."

Leo is following Millie but is clearly not following mentally what she says. Aware of his confusion she stops, turns and looks straight into his eyes.

"Is it clear?"

"As mud."

Millie takes a deep breath: it's her moment now.

"It means Nic's set you up: he'll say that you took it... and that you made him believe I did."

35

"He might have sent someone just to make sure I've popped you."

"Why do that Leo? He trusts you, you know… t-r-u-s-t."

"What if nobody's at the car? R-I-P, sister."

"Someone was following us earlier; they didn't look like Jehovah's witnesses to me."

"I saw nothing."

"You were too busy looking up my skirt."

"I was checking a working girl's trade secret."

"You really are the working part of an arsehole Leo."

Leo thrusts his hand forward gripping Millie by the neck.

"Best of luck back at the car, sweetheart."

A long knife flicks open under Millie's nose.

"But not too much."

The forest is a kaleidoscope of light bouncing on leaves, a silent and magic witness to Millie and Leo wondering through it to get back to the car.

As they climb up a steep path, mud and slippery rocks make the ascending uneasy especially for Millie, who's finding her way grabbing bushes and branches to pull herself up. Just behind her Leo is climbing with ease giggling as he's enjoying the view of Millie's posterior inches from his nose.

Whack!

A thick branch has just hit his nose and killed any humour from his face.

Crack!

A second and stronger blow sends him down into the mud, sliding on his back.

Millie is holding the branch looking down at Leo, it is quite surprising so much strength is packed into such a little frame, but adrenaline mixed with a strong survival instinct are powerful enough.

Millie is hysterically triumphant: "Lucky strike!"

She jumps on top of Leo's chest, sitting on it, legs spread pointing her knees to the ground. She takes the gun out of his pocket.

We see in close up Leo's face, covered with blood and mud.

Millie's voice is heard off screen: "A mud mask isn't enough to improve your shit face, Leo."

Millie's face is now breathing down Leo's neck, like a lioness smelling her prey. The gun barrel is now right under his chin. He's muttering something incomprehensible, gargling blood.

Millie has found her sense of humour again: "Ever considered plastic surgery?"

The barrel slowly moving up to Leo's nose

"Maybe Nic trusts you, but he doesn't trust me, his Millie, that's why they were following us."

Millie pushes the barrel up Leo's nostrils: "Do I smell burn... or you're shitting yourself?"

Boom!

On the edge of the woods two men are leaning against a car. A second car is not far away parked near a fence, Leo's car, the passenger door left open.

The two men are seen from the back: the one on the left is bald and bold, in his late forties. The other is much younger with long hair. They're Nic's men, dangerous and impatient. Alex, the long haired man speaks first

"Did you hear that?"

Boom! A second shot echoes in the distance.

"Kev? You've-"

"Knock it off Alex! I hear better than you without all that fluff around the ears that makes you so cool."

"What took Leo so long? Doesn't he wake up with a hard on?"

"Nah, not Leo, his idea of fun is another kind of penetration: the lead or steel one, he's sick."

The forest returns to its silence. Alex struggles to light a cigarette in the gentle breeze. He throws it away with a frustrated flick of his fingers.

"Kev, are you positive about-"

"Flat out. Nic was specific."

Kevin moves away towards the fence unzipping his trousers to take a piss.

Deep into the forest we now see Leo's bloodied body lying in the mud with only his underwear on.

Millie is moving fast, wearing Leo's clothes and boots. She has recovered his sunglasses and the hat. She's now looking at him holding the knife.

Her face is cleaned up of the mud and of any emotion, while observing what's left of Leo's face: not much, especially his well-groomed moustache.

She bites her lip thinking, then she moves to a near tree trunk, collecting some resin pouring out the wood using Leo's knife.

She applies the sticky matter under her nose.

She then takes a deep breath as if getting high.

With a content smile she throws her head back, the gold of the resin shining in the morning light.

She suddenly falls on her knees, next to Leo's abdomen. We see her face in disgust as she's lowering Leo's pants, waving the knife.

"No wonder your gun was so big Leo."

From her movements we understand she's cutting something.

A bunch of Leo's pubic hair appears in her fingers. She's looking at it amused.

"Does this make me a dickhead?"

Giggling about her own joke she applies the hair to the resin under her nose, the result is hair-raising good.

"Best of luck sweetheart."

We see Kevin and Alex back in their positions, near the car. They still have their back to the camera.

Alex has some headphones in, listening to loud acid music. Alex whacks him on the shoulder.

"Alex! Get that shit off. When you see a couple of moustaches on a dickhead coming out of the trees shave them."

"I thought Nic trusted Leo."

"Nic gives a fuck about Leo."

"What about the money?"

"Fuck that too, that's petty cash for him, he wants to set an example."

Silence. There is only the wind blowing Alex's hair.

"Kev, suppose for a moment, ok, that Millie out-smarts Leo."

"And my hair grows back."

"No, no, c'mon Kev: you've said Millie's quite a type. Let's say today's her lucky day."

"Her very lucky day."

"Whatever, but she makes it."

"What are you getting at Alex?"

"She tells us where the dosh is and we let her go."

Kevin is listening carefully.

"Leo making compost, Millie making for South America, Nic's happy, make my day!"

"Alex, Alex.. I'll give it some heavy thought ok?"

"Wanna pillow? C'mon man, could be our lucky number coming up from those woods."

"It's Leo."

Kevin says it while cocking his gun.

"What?"

"You heard me, are you blind as well as deaf? Over there, Leo's coming out of the trees. I guess nobody got lucky today."

With very fast sharp movements they both reach for their guns. The sound of triggers being cocked precedes the blur of the violent sound of their machine guns.

We fade to black in a hail of bullets as the end credits roll in.

3. SHE-FI

I have always had a soft spot for science fiction, especially when rooted in reasonably realistic surroundings, not Star Trek stuff though, sorry guys.

The idea for this short screenplay began when I was a kid and I remember playing in an abandoned factory and once finding this comic book that was obviously a rush print of some sort. It had a lot of typing and spelling mistakes and the drawings were not that brilliant but for some odd reason I always thought there was a possible story in it that could blossom eventually.

When I was asked to write something with some element of surreal science the starting point was the memory of that precious find.

The script ended up to quite an advanced state of pre-production, concept drawings were made, storyboards drawn and quite a bit of work went into the project.

A fabulous cast was found who performed some good test readings and locations were scouted successfully, but as so often happens someone along the line changed his mind and the project was shelved.

I still like it, even though it was written quite few years ago.

Fade in

We are in a large abandoned factory, it is late afternoon.

Two men are running in the distance, back lit against the huge windows. The sound of their steps echoing is interrupted by one of them shouting to the other.

"Is it safe? Is it safe?"

They both stop at the same time, breathing heavily. Elvis is rather handsome with dark hair and a pale complexion: sleek and skinny wearing a dark suit, the cool dude type. He's holding a gun that seems too heavy in his almost feminine hand. He speaks in a fast but rather petulant way.

"Is it safe? Kurt?"

Kurt is quite tall, strongly built, the hardly talking type, a face that has seen things we don't want to know about.

Tough and mean like the sawn off shotgun he's holding with absolute nonchalance. He's also wearing black, but more as an occupational requirement, so blood doesn't show.

Elvis asks again the same question.

"Is it-"

"Shut up Elvis-king-of-all-fuck-ups. 'Is it safe?' You sound just like that bitch friend of yours, you asshole!"

Elvis seems genuinely surprised.

"Fanny-the-bitch a friend of mine? Now that's offensive. I hardly knew her."

"Funny you say that. If it wasn't for her broken heart we wouldn't be in this mess. Shut up now."

Elvis is definitely not the silent type

"You shouldn't have killed her. But I guess you have to be Kurt. Is that your real name? Do you guys use a pen name, gun-name type of thing?"

Kurt is trying not to listen to Elvis' nonsense.

Elvis insists.

"Kurt, what kind of name is that? How do I spell it?"

"Correctly. Now shut the fuck up."

Silence at last. Kurt looks around assessing the situation with the confidence of someone who has been chased before, and got away with it.

"It's too quiet, I don't like it."

Elvis chirps in again trying to be funny.

"You told me to keep quiet."

Kurt shoots an angry look at Elvis.

"Hey Kurt, c'mon chill out man, just joking. I always talk when I'm nervous."

"You always talk, like a Thai hooker. We'll stay here for a while, it's a good spot."

We see the place from Kurt's point of view: empty boxes, old machinery, grease and dirt. Industrial decadence. Elvis is having a look around as well.

"This place gives me the creeps. You scared? Kurt?"

We see Kurt's scarred face: fear looks completely out of place there.

"Kurt! I mean not even scared of dying? Everybody's scared of something, especially of death."

"Death in your case will be a relief, so I don't have to listen to your shit anymore."

Elvis seems slightly offended.

"I'm serious: we're talking about life and death here. My life and my death."

"So? It's not like Manchester United has lost."

"Great! I feel like throwing up and you feed me with sick football jokes. Thanks Kurt."

Silence. Elvis collects himself.

"What's this place anyway?"

"A printing company."

"What makes you say that?"

"A fuckin' huge sign on the roof, genius. Now can you do without tour guide or baby-sitter and let daddy check out Disneyland here?"

Sulking, Elvis stomps off leaving Kurt to do his exploring. A poster of a naked girl on a column nearby catches Kurt's attention. He puts his right hand behind it and tears the paper with his index finger, making it appear on the printed bimbo's private parts.

"Fanny fuckin' freak of yours."

Kurt turns towards Elvis to verify the effect of his joke, finding Elvis busy reading a magazine.

"Don't wank over it you'll need the energy later."

"This is great stuff, man."

"What did you find, Playboy with odourama centrefold?"

"Better: this is state of the art sci-fi. The sort of stuff that can make your brain pop."

Kurt quickly glances at the pages.

"Is it a bird? Is it a plane? No it's a flying faggot!"

"This ain't no superman, this is much better, it's kinda real. Superman got on my tits the day I saw him stopping a bullet shot by the bad guy and spitting it back using his teeth: c'mon!"

Kurt is incredulous: "Hey, you buy that a guy who looks like a condom full of nuts can fly but it bothers you that he stops bullets with his fillings? My jaw stopped a bullet once, no big deal."

"It's not the lead biting that bothers me, it's the spitting it back at the bad guy. It's kinda... arrogant."

Kurt's clearly not following, Elvis is even to keen to elucidate.

"Ok: sci-fi, science fiction. Good guys fighting bad guys or some freak experiment gone wrong, but real people, you know. It's fiction but it's kinda real. Something that could happen in the future with science playing a major part: time machine, genetic manipulation, robots, third dimension, alien stuff."

"Flying fuckin' saucers."

"Cool dudes and babes with hi-tech attitude."

"You better beam down and get real, Capt. Kirk."

Elvis brings the magazine under Kurt's nose, important evidence to make his point.

"Look: here you have a guy crashing a door, not flying through it."

We see what Kurt is seeing, a black and white drawing of what Elvis just described, with a big crash effect word standing out.

Crash!

A loud crash echoes followed by the sound of glass shattering. Kurt jolts, shotgun ready: "He's here, son of a sick bitch."

A second noise, like wood being smashed, is heard coming from a different direction.

"More puppies from a sick litter"

Kurt is now looking at his shotgun with a grim expression. He puts his hand in his pocket. As he takes it out only a few bullets remain on his palm.

He turns to Elvis.

"Fuck! Elvis?"

Elvis is still absorbed by his reading; Kurt picks up a book from a pile of junk nearby and throws a perfect hit at Elvis.

"Check your hardware instead of jerking off your brain on that shit."

"Sci-fi."

Kurt springs to his feet and points the shotgun at Elvis's neck. Elvis turns to him; a big Cheshire cat grin appearing on his face. Kurt might as well be pointing a bar of chocolate.

"Check your fuckin' gun!"

Elvis smiles even more.

"I knew you were going to say that, I knew the exact words, I knew what you were going to do before you did it!"

Kurt is not amused.

"No shit. So you know I have a bad feeling about this."

Elvis points at the magazine: "Wrong, this is our way out."

Elvis is waving the magazine at a very pissed off Kurt.

"What's wrong with you shithead! They're going to pigeon shoot at us and you play prophet?"

Kurt lowers his shotgun in despair.

"Gimme the heavy-metal."

A long silence follows Kurt's words.

Elvis is staring at Kurt with a strange expression painted on his face, some sort of resignation.

"It's empty."

Kurt's jaw drops

"What? You never fired."

"I never loaded it."

"Come again."

"It's empty: no bullets, zilch, nothing, nada, nil, naught. I hate guns; I'm into software, not hardware, that's why I hired you to help me get out with this stuff. It was meant to be clean: in-out.. No pain, all gain. I assumed Fanny was on my side, not batting for both teams."

"You stupid fuck, assumption is the mother of all fuck-ups. I assumed that the gun was loaded; now I'm fucked. You expect to steal superfuckinfreakinsecret experiment government data and have people laying red carpets in front of you just because you flash an empty gun? The government wants your ass, the mob wants your ass, every bad-ass wants your ass so badly that when they've finished with you they'll carve "Elvis-rotten-pelvis" on your tombstone."

Elvis breaks into tears, terrified, he sobs quietly.

"Yeah, get religious."

"What am I gonna do?"

"Talk them to death. Just don't talk and don't think from now on, just keep reading the fucking magazine, you crazy asshole."

As Kurt looks around for a way out Elvis dives into his magazine, mumbling to himself.

"I'm not crazy, it's all in here, word by word, every action."

Elvis looks at the cover of the magazine.

"This must be at least ten years old but the date on the cover it's today's! This very day!"

Kurt answers without even looking.

"Bad day, fuck it."

Elvis suddenly comes to life

"Listen Kurt, I know this is crazy shit but everything that happened since this morning is here, with some variations."

"Knock it off."

"Kurt-"

"Don't Kurt me, I don't like being Kurted."

"Ok, ok, but listen: it's not easy to follow this. There are a lot of misprints, captions in the wrong strips, spelling mistakes but I swear it's amazing. Funny huh?"

"I'm laughing so hard I'll choke."

Elvis start reading: "I'm laughing so hard I'll choke."

Kurt jumps to hit Elvis who's already running away as if he knew in advance Kurt's move.

Kurt runs after him, shouting: "I'll kick this shit back into your crazy ass."

"Listen to me!"

"I'll make you choke in it!"

Elvis is talking and running: "Think, if I'm talking shit, how would I know you're going to trip over in a second?"

Kurt's face is as red as chilly pepper

"Fuck you!"

We freeze frame on Kurt's raged expression. For a split second it looks drawn cartoon style.

Then as we go back to real action we see Kurt as he slips and falls on some boxes. Elvis stops nearby.

Both men are breathing heavily. Elvis has found a confidence unknown to him before.

He is almost triumphant: "Fuck you fuck boy you see. I told you, here, you can see what happens next."

Elvis hands over the magazine to Kurt, who pushes it away.

"Ok, tell me, tell me what happens next, so I can do the opposite."

"Why are you such a tight ass, loosen up."

Elvis starts flicking through the magazine, he talks fast.

"This is how it starts: two men running, one is shouting 'is it safe?' please stop me when it sounds familiar."

"A fucking coincidence."

"Maybe, but we don't really have much to lose if we follow what is in here."

Kurt gets up, collecting his shotgun.

"Ok, what's next in the crystal ball?"

"Hhmm, here it is: 'suddenly the silence is broken by the sound of fun' it reads-"

From the distance loud music is heard, it seems somebody is having a party. Kurt looks nervous, Elvis puzzled.

"Doesn't make sense, I'm sure it's meant to be 'gun'!

Oh, sure, it must be 'the sound of a gun being fired', shit..."

Elvis is now looking at a red laser dot moving on the page of the magazine, the laser that comes from a gun's aim system.

Boom! A gunshot to make anyone deaf, while Kurt is already jumping behind boxes firing back.

For some very long seconds a hell of gunshots breaks loose with bullets peppering everything.

In all this havoc Elvis remains still where he is, right in the middle, holding the magazine.

A fluorescent fixture gets hit just above him and swings down: the oscillating light makes the scene change from reality to an identical one drawn as a comic strip.

In all this mayhem Kurt keeps firing and jumps out of his hideout pushing the frozen Elvis to safety. They manage to get to the next floor down through a narrow metal staircase. Kurt is not impressed.

"You and your fucking story, don't you like happy endings?"

Elvis looks at Kurt with spirited expression. He is very calm.

"You believe me now. I couldn't be hit, because it was drawn that way. Every shade, the slightest nuance."

Kurt can't believe this guy is for real.

"Fuck you and fuck your fuckin' story. These people have a volume deal with the obituary and you want to lecture them in fine art?"

Kurt hits the magazine Elvis is still holding, making it fly right into a pond of dirty water.

"Fuck you, written or not written."

Elvis picks up the wet magazine, finding with some difficulty the right page. He reads slowly from the page.

"Fuck you, written or not written."

Kurt shakes his head hopelessly and looks out of a window on his left.

"We must get the fuck out of here before I go out of my mind."

"I'll get to the car."

"Car? What car?"

"It's here: it's drawn like a spaceship but I'm sure it will turn up as a car." Elvis shows the page to Kurt.

"You don't give up do you? There's no space-car, arse-hole."

Elvis goes to a nearby door leading to a staircase.

"I knew you were going to say that. I'll call you on your mobile from the phone in the car. Switch it on, I've got the number."

Elvis disappears leaving a stressed out Kurt behind.

A few moments of silence follow then Kurt seems struck by a sudden thought.

He now checks his pocket; as he takes his hand out we see he's holding a mobile phone.

"How the hell?"

Kurt switches the phone on. Silence, there is only the sound of dripping water somewhere.

Then a feeble ring is heard, followed by another one. Kurt answers his phone.

"It's you. What? No, nothing, door? What door?"

Suddenly a door on his right bursts open and a man in a dark coat follows, shooting right, left and centre with a machine gun.

Kurt flies down the staircase where Elvis has disappeared earlier.

As he reaches the bottom of the stairs he finds himself in a large littered area: the ground floor of the factory.

A huge shutter goes up revealing a frantic Elvis shouting in Kurt's direction: "Run!"

Kurt runs following Elvis into the courtyard. A car is parked in the middle.

Elvis is still holding his precious magazine.

"Now you believe me!"

"Cut the shit."

Kurt jumps into the driver's seat.

The body of a dead man in the passenger seat falls on him. There is a bloody mess where the face should be.

"Fuck, fuck!"

Kurt pushes the body towards the opposite door, as Elvis sits in the back still looking at the magazine.

Kurt is now fiddling with the wiring under the steering wheel.

Elvis comes to the rescue once more: "Look in his space suit, in his suit I mean."

Kurt finds the car keys after a quick search of the dead man's suit.

As he turns the key, the engine sputters but doesn't start. Not a good day.

"What now, what's next, son of a bitch?"

Elvis is trying to decipher what's left of the magazine.

"The woman in the back seat glances at the rear mirror. The woman?"

Elvis glances at the mirror. A woman's face is reflected. She has Elvis's features but is definitely a woman.

Kurt by now has lost his cool. Without looking at Elvis he opens the car door, shouting.

"Fucked, we're fucked. Get out of here!"

They both get out of the car from the same side, as Kurt turns to Elvis we can see the most surprised expression his face has ever experienced. Where did that woman in a little black number come from?

"Who the hell?"

Boom! Boooom!

Kurt is hit twice in the chest. He very slowly sits on the ground, his expression hasn't changed.

Bang!

A third bullet hits Kurt on his forehead. He falls on his back in no time.

Two men are running towards Elvis, or what is now his female version.

Rob is a big-bellied menace holding a machine gun as if he sleeps with it. Dan has dark hair; he's wearing a dark coat, holding a sniper rifle with laser system. His golden earring shines on his left ear. Both of them stop next to the car.

Rob's voice is deep: "Relax lady, the cavalry's here."

He looks in the car cautiously, then gently kicks Kurt's body pointing the gun at Kurt's head, just in case.

"He's very dead. All cool. Let's see what we've got here."

He grabs the magazine from Elvis's hand, shaking it as if something could be hidden inside."

"Nothing, where the fuck is it?"

Dan pats down the woman who we used to know as Elvis.

"What's your name sweetheart?"

Elvis is in a double shock: as Dan pats him down he feels his new assets. In search of an answer he looks at the dead body of his partner

"Fa... Fanny."

"What a sweet name, do you read this stuff?"

Rob is waving the magazines at Elvis, now called Fanny, who nods automatically.

Rob flicks through some pages.

"It's all crap; you don't believe this shit do you? You're a practical girl."

Rob gets to the last page

"Look, a happy ending: our heroine leaves the planet without a scar. Heart-warming. Really, I feel weepy."

Whack! With a fast movement Rob shuts the magazine. He then turns to Dan who has a chilling smile on his face. Fanny seems absolutely terrified.

Rob asks sweetly, but in a chilling way: "Did you know these guys?"

Fanny shakes her head negatively.

Rob is charming like a snake. "You know, a gem like you, if I had the time I'd take you out, hold your hand, kiss you on the cheek. Watch the stars."

Rob eyes Dan with perfect understanding: it's a game they must play often.

He carries on.

"I know it sounds rude, but don't fuck with me now, I'm not in the mood and when I'm on the rag I'm not my true self."

"So, do you know these guys?"

Fanny shakes her head again

"Are you sure? No connection, relationship, romance, exchange of bodily fluids?"

Fanny keeps shaking her head in desperate denial, eyes glued to Kurt's dead body.

"You shouldn't be all broken up over that scumbag. Nobody will miss him, and I'll get a medal for not missing him."

A big smile follows his words. He looks at the magazine again.

"Sci-fi... ok: let's talk hi-tech. Have you seen a floppy disc, you know kind of stiff-square-thing? Look at me!"

A long silence follows: Rob's eyes looking straight into the woman's soul.

"Guess not, only lots of floppy dicks."

He takes a pause for effect, enjoying his pathetic humour, then he gives the magazine back to Fanny.

"If you believe this shit I can believe you. Get lost before I change my mind on the happy ending."

Fanny starts walking away, not quite sure he's going to let her go. One of the high heels is missing adding discomfort to an already uncomfortable situation.

Rob shouts after her: "Hey, Fanny-love!"

Fanny freezes for what seems like an eternity.

"Show me that stuff again, just the cover."

Fanny holds the magazine towards Rob.

We see the cover of the magazine in greater detail; the title 'she-fi' is written in big letters.

The hyper realistic illustration of a busty heroine in a sexy space suit completes the cover.

"Is that how you spell sci-fi?"

Fade to black; the end credits roll in as Rob's words are echoing in the courtyard.

4. FADE TO BLACK

The following shorts, except 'Roadkill', are part of what is called in film jargon a Rogopag, a film that contains different short films grouped together, shot by different directors.

Each short film was supposed to be almost a confession to camera, with more or less grotesque results. Every piece starts with a caption on screen, normally a famous quote, to set the mood.

The film as a whole was titled "Personal exposures" and the general theme was that all sections should be confessions to camera, in any case something that we are not meant to watch, or something that would make the viewer uncomfortable.

Only one of these shorts, 'fade to black', was actually produced as a short film. The final result was not bad, but not the way it was intended.

I guess that is something any writer should be prepared to, without getting too uncomfortable about it.

A caption appears on black screen:

HISTORY IS A SET OF LIES AGREED UPON

(Napoleon Bonaparte)

The image on screen looks like it is projected from an old and weathered black and white film. We can make out one chair in the middle of a bare room; it is the only object in sight. A bare bulb casts little light on the four walls: not a friendly looking place.

Suddenly a big black woman, in her late 50s, appears sitting on the chair, as if this film has been put together by somebody who's surely no film editor.

She seems amused by the experience. Her voice is warm and jolly. She giggles quite often; a contagious laugh follows.

"Is it OK here? Can you see me? Can you really squeeze my big black ass all inside that tiny black box? Ah, science! Our fathers used to sing at the moon, now our sons are landing on it, spoiling everything. Ah the good old times. But I guess all old times seem good. So, when can we start? What? You've started already? Oh I like that! Simple."

She clears her throat.

"Today's the 11th July 1969, my name is Mariam with one 'A' after the first 'M' and one before the last one. All the girls of my village were called so; maybe all the girls in Ethiopia had this name at that time... 1915. I was born near Addis Ababa; my father had been an Ascari in the Italian Army and had a little pension so we've been raised quite decently. I'm here now, doing this, because I have to secure my secret somehow and this is the only way. I am hoping that one day people will believe what I have to say."

She pauses slightly, adjusting herself on the chair, taking a deep breath.

"I was Mussolini's mistress for some time. Yeah, M-u-s-s-o-l-i-n-i, bald fella who ruled Italy for twenty years. I know, I know, everyone knows I'm black and I have to say that I'm not terribly self-conscious about it. I'm black and I have decided I like my colour a long time ago and so did he. Mussolini didn't mind because he was colour blind. Not many people know that and that's thanks to me. Until he met me he always thought that his black shirted mates were all dressed in virginal white.. like cherubs during Creation. It all started on a Sunday morning... 1936. Every Sunday I used to go to a pond near my village to swim. You had to be careful because crocodiles like to swim there as well. So I was just about to get in as God created me, when I saw him, not God you silly! Mussolini! Not too sharply because I've always been short-sighted, but blimey! He was magnificent, on his white horse, dressed in a very elegant grey uniform and a shiny helmet.

Well I thought it was his helmet but as he came closer I noticed he was bald as an ostrich's egg. I couldn't make head or tail out of half of what he said, but it sounded nice. I knew he was lost because he had the above-the-eye-look that people have when they're lost, drunk or dead."

She stops, pensive.

"Mmh, I suppose he could have been drunk. Anyway as we were exploring each other, not an easy task with all those medals, a crocodile turned his horse into a sea horse: no legs, just the head on top of the tail. Luckily my father had a mule that was part of his payoff from his service... or so he let us believe anyway. So I went back to fetch the poor animal. My mother was there: she had been a beautiful woman, when young, but now her skin was so cracked and withered that it was hard to spot her against a wall of mud. I told her that I was leaving because I've met a very interesting man. She said he had to be very interesting to make me change village. He's interesting all right I replied, but she shook her head and grunted: 'I'll believe it when I see it'. I was furious: 'You wouldn't know an interesting man if he floated in the air and pissed in your face!' I shouted. 'Is that what he's been doing?' Her answer wiped off any further doubt or late remorse I could have ever had. As I was pulling the stubborn animal towards the pond, I noticed the great 'Duce' being given a lift by a passing German tank... he was so handsome with his bald head shining out of the turret. The shine guided me to his camp, as a providential comet. I guess you call it love at first sight. But at the sight of me entering his tent he called me a whore, and tried to send me away. But I stood tough and said: 'You dislike me because I'm not one of those white tarts you exploit. I have a mind of my own and I have a body of my own that doesn't fit into the preconceived patterns men like you dictate."

She pauses smiling.

"-You mean you are black-, he said baffled. Well I don't know if it was this or the word I used: 'dictate', he liked that. Realising he was colour blind was quite a shock for him: for many years he had been drinking red wine thinking it was white. That really bothered him. He hated red, any red. So he took me to Italy,

Rome, and told me my job was telling him the true colour of things. That turned up being a hell of a job: everything there was black and gold, like a pack of John Player Special. He took my advice on many issues, including getting rid of the eagle-shaped bidet taps in his bathroom. A lot of people always thought he had a big Ego but in fact he tolerated different opinions... unless they were too different from his own. You see... he was a very insecure person: consider his famous speeches always beginning with 'Italiani!' just to remind himself who he was talking to. He even followed my advice to convince Hitler that Italy was a reliable ally: we all know the rest of the story. In private he was not the macho figure of the propaganda: things like 'IT'S BETTER TO DIE ON YOUR FEET THAN TO LIVE ON YOUR KNEES' came to him only because he suffered arthritis. He was a lonely man. He used to say: dictatorship gives you pleasure but like masturbation is a lonely business. "

She stops, almost puzzled.

"Probably that's why you never see a woman dictator, we don't play with ourselves much, or maybe because when a man gets up to speak people listen, then look (Hitler wasn't exactly Gary Cooper, was he?). When a woman gets up, people look and if they like what they see, they listen, pity that Marilyn Monroe didn't have much to say."

She stops, the chair feels even more uncomfortable now; she stretches her back with a grin.

"I'm not trying to depict him as a holy figure but don't forget we have such a bad perception of the devil because God has written all the books. Mussolini was more into making butter than cannons. He once organised a banquet for his officers going to conquer Greece. When he had to change plans because there was no petrol for the tanks, he made another banquet to celebrate their staying. He always said 'food is the only thing you can take with you when you die'. I was next to him even in those last moments (it would have been really embarrassing if his socks were of two different colours!). As he was facing the firing squad I told him: 'They don't hate you, they hate your uniform!' And his last words were: 'Yes, but there's me inside!' I hope someone will believe my story. I met Hitler's secret lover at the time, a beautiful black boy from Nigeria, and he confessed to me he was keeping diaries of everything, but he feared that nobody would have ever believed these diaries were authentic. Maybe it's true, even black on white fades with time: all colours fade, like memories. I don't know if the world is ready for my story yet, but maybe... one day... maybe on a Sunday."

Her contagious big laugh follows as the end credits roll in and we fade to black.

4. READY WHEN YOU ARE

If there is one thing that embarrasses almost anyone is to see your mum or dad doing something really
gross, it is something most people cannot face.

What about if you did not see your dad for many
years and suddenly you receive a tape with something
a bit hard to digest recorded on it.

Well, you are just about to find out.

A caption appears on black screen:

A MAN IS A MAN IS A MAN

A second caption appears slowly underneath:

ONLY AS LONG AS HE CAN

The opening shots start full of flares and scratches,
showing what an amateur 8" film is: amateurish.

We see the blurred figure of someone fiddling with the camera; a hissing sound is heard together with the unnerving thump of a microphone being hit.

Suddenly the image becomes sharp, revealing someone with a stocking pulled down over his face, like a bank robber. We can see he's talking to the camera but no sound is heard.

Abruptly we hear his voice, as if he suddenly managed to get the microphone to work:

"- difficult to face but necessary. I'm sorry about this (he pinches the stocking) but I have to take you through it gradually and I thought this may prepare you a bit, softening things up. I've read somewhere once that glamour photographers, I think one says glamour, you know, the ones who screw long legged girls and then sell their pictures shortly after as art, well those apparently use stockings. Not cheap stuff but Dior like this one, all to achieve that beautiful look."

He stops suddenly, realising he is muttering a lot of nonsense.

"Pathetic isn't it, a pitiful facade. I better stop fooling about and get straight to the point. I'll take this off, but first I'll dim the light in here, it's too bright."

He tampers with a nearby lamp.

Suddenly all the lights go off. We can hear him muttering something in the dark. The wick flame of his lighter allows us to see his masked face again.

"Sorry your dad has never been good at this, the DIY thing, so where were we… My memory is not as good as it used to be, all those chemicals, those drugs! But yes, the mask (sighs), let's go through this once and for all, for your sake."

He lights a nearby candle with the lighter, then takes the stocking off his head. A cascade of blonde hair falls out. Heavy make up shines in the dim light. Dad is now a 'she'.

"Do you recognise me? Did mum show you any pictures of me? I hope so…I was very handsome you know, maybe… Let's see."

He fiddles with the lamp, the light comes back. He blows out the candle.

"Here, let me come closer, don't be afraid."

He smiles horrendously enough to frighten a pit-bull to death.

"Oh, those eyes! I just came out of the clinic. I hated it! Oh no! I'm well, I just needed a little adjustment, I'm not a teenager anymore you know, but I still look the part, don't you think?"

He puts his hands under his breasts to give more evidence.

"You see? No bra, how many people of my age can say that? Uh and a flat belly too. I think it's disgusting to see men or women with those huge (mimes a large stomach) Aahrgh... Terrible! So what do you think? Futuristic, huh? It's amazing what science can do today... miracles! It hasn't been easy... not at the time I have done it. The first, can you imagine? The very first, aren't you proud of me? I know it must have been hard for you, but think of me, it has been hell.

I would do it again, I had no choice, but if I did, no media, they are horrible monsters feeding on my flesh. Did you see my skin how fab? Still soft even after all these years, the right hormones are the secret, I think... look, a baby's bottom."

He accompanies the last words caressing his arm. He then sings softly a well known baby powder jingle, then:

"Gosh! I should stop doing this, these awful TV ads: prehistoric. People might guess my age. How old are you now? Seventeen? Eighteen? Ah what a wonderful age."

He stops, picks up a hanky from his handbag, blows his nose loudly.

"I know, you're right, I'm changing the subject, I should be talking about me. there's so much I want to tell you! So, after the first operation I just changed, you know. Well I've never liked it. It's so ugly. I don't know if you have seen one ever in the flesh, horrible little thing, actually I say little but mine was quite a presence, I could have made a donkey jealous! Oh shit, I swear like a truck driver, sorry, that comes from too much time with them, all those long journeys, I was trying to put some money together for the operation."

He stares blankly at the camera for few seconds.

"They all left me, your mum first, she was two months pregnant with you sweetheart and thinking that she didn't want to have a baby! I did, I wanted a little girl. So, lost my job, friends, everything. I've spent nine months on the streets doing, you know, FUCK!"

He suddenly grabs his right ear as if feeling some intense pain.

"One of the stitches is gone! That Brazilian asshole, the plastic surgeon, he said my skin was too thick, now look, what a disaster!"

He grabs the camera with both hands, checking the damage using the reflective quality of the camera lens as a mirror: a rather grotesque and disturbing image.

"Uhmm, not too baaad, it could have been worse. So, where were we? Ah the operation! It went well, everyone was very nice to me, there was this doctor, very handsome, who painted my body with wild colours: I ended up looking like one of those posters you see in the butcher's, a poor cow cut up into joints, and this cute doctor made me giggle. I'm so ticklish! He was drawing on my 'best end' and I was enjoying it so much I didn't want to go to sleep. When I woke up I was all covered in bandages like a mummy and all these people asking me all these questions, how do I feel, if I feel different, as if something is missing, (sighs) believe me, it was horrible, they were horrible, raping me verbally."

He pauses sadly.

"After I left I met this Count, a naughty man, naughty but a true gentleman, he never touched me. I was still in some pain, and full of stitches. I told him that I had a caesarean, and lost the baby as well. He believed it, he trusted me; he was so sweet! He died of a heart attack two months later when he found out, some pig journalist rang asking what a Count was doing with someone without a cunt. The old man didn't find it funny and had a fit, and left me rich! So I went a bit wild, lots of boyfriends, you know men, or maybe you don't, but believe me they all want only one thing, your money!"

He shrugs and adjusts his position.

"So years go by and I wanted to see how you were getting along. You were only six then, and such a pretty girl. You were so quiet, I know they told you I was some eccentric auntie from down under, they said you were still too young to understand, it could have been a shock they said. If it was up to me I would have told you then: one bam, shock treatment. I mean, you know what I mean. So quiet you were, not like your step-brother, you know he's not your real brother, don't you? Your mother remarried while she was still pregnant, the merry widow! Life is a bitch so is she, anyway your so-called brother, whatever his name, the little monster."

He gestures indicating something small in size, with a mocking expression on his face.

"A dwarf with a big mouth. The house was full of people, relatives, friends, the lot. It was near Christmas, of course I didn't buy him a present, why should I? Only the one for you, sweetheart, oh I can't remember now, it was, expensive (lowering his voice) I remember that. (Pauses.) So he starts jumping around me, your monster-brother, shouting with his squeaky voice." He adjust himself and then speaks imitating a squeaky voice: "One, two, guess who, three, four, knock at the door, five, six, hide your dick, seven,

eight, take your mate, nine, ten, old auntie again!"
Aaargh! I would have squashed the little maggot! I
can't stand that word: old! How dare he! As a result
everyone was now staring at me, especially your
"daddy" (sarcastic), not that I can remember much of
him, no, nothing to do with chemicals, owing more to
the fact that he's such an insignificant man, a perfect
nothing, the only thing he perfected! He was a real
hunk, good at drinking beer and always talking about
motorbikes. And what would you expect from somebody who needs lots of cc between his legs to feel
something? I can't understand your mother, he must
have the IQ of a gorilla. How she could end up with
him, after what I've, well.. the past is a funny place,
things seem different there. I'm a bit of a poet you
know, I still write, I might have something for you
right here."

He looks into his bag nearby: all sorts of bizarre
paraphernalia comes out. Finally a little black book appears in his hands. He opens it religiously, mumbles
something as if reading something of no importance,
then solemnly:

"Here it is, hermetic and powerful as I remembered"
He clears his voice, takes his time, looking inspired.
"Don't forget not to forget."

There is silence. His expression reflects the emptiness of what he just declaimed. He probably realises that sometimes what is written is not as good as you think once spoken out loud.

"Humm, well I thought I would read it to you anyway, so many years have gone past, but I still feel and look young and I think we should spend some time together. You've never answered my letters. I have a feeling that your mother is intercepting them, that's why I'm doing this piece to camera so you can see with your own eyes, and hear what I have to say and I do have a lot to tell you."

He stops, sobbing.

"I'm still your father!"

He's quite upset and his gesticulating makes the lamp fall over, the scene blacks out. The pale flame of the lighter brings him back to us on the screen, his face in grotesque bewilderment.

"Am I?"

Fade to black, the end credits roll in.

5. BODY DOUBLE

I have in this case kept the original screenplay format slightly more true to the original; there are many quick dialogue exchanges that work better if you have an immediate grasp of who is saying what.

The following story came to me when I heard of a couple who had their home videotaped sex exploits broadcasted to an entire town when one of their naughty tapes went live by mistake on a local television.

I always thought that it would be funny to reconstruct what and how it happened. Sex can be funny, really funny.

Black screen.

We hear some noises as if someone is fumbling with the microphone.

A caption slowly appears:

THE MOST EXCITING THING IS TO BE
SPECTATOR OF YOUR OWN PERFORMANCE

The caption disappears revealing a middle class bedroom: it contains dark furniture, Klimt's 'Kiss' reproduction hanging on a wall, a dark duvet on the bed, designer's lamp and a phone on one side, a stereo system on the other.

A man's voice is heard off screen, his name is Danny.

"Oh come on Sandy, just this once! C'mon! What's the big deal?"

Sandy's answer is also heard off screen, almost hysterical.

"Danny! You can't ask me to do it like that, I'm not a-"

"A what? I didn't say or even think anything. That's you making things up! I've never-"

"OK, OK, doesn't make any difference. I feel embarrassed that's all."

"Embarrassed? For what reason honey? It's just the two of us! It's no different from what we usually do, it's just that this time there's a camera!"

"That's it! You've said it. I can't do it knowing that there will be people watching."

"Are you serious? Who on earth will be watching? It's just for us, to add some spice to our relationship, fan the flames of passion."

"It ain't fun! I don't feel like it even if nobody is watching. I'm embarrassed! I'm not Julia Roberts you know."

"Just for the record Julia Roberts used a body double in the naked scenes of Pretty Woman. Sandy, you do have a beautiful body, you're very pretty and sexy and I want to capture that. Do you remember when I filmed your sister's wedding and you said how beautiful she looked on screen? And she's not exactly a beauty queen in the flesh. Can you imagine what I am gonna make you look like? Like bloody Garbo if you excuse me."

There's a moment of silence. Then the sound of high heels on the floor is heard. Sandy is almost thrown into the scene by Danny.

She's not exactly a beauty, around thirty-five, brunette, quite plump, petite, more an estate agent's secretary than a glamorous model. She looks quite uncomfortable and the tight frock she's wearing doesn't make things easier for her. She looks straight at the camera almost in a panic.

"Oh my God, I don't believe I'm doing this! Danny, is that thing on?" (she is pointing at the camera).

"No it's not. I'll switch it on once you've warmed up. I don't want to waste tape."

"But why is that little red light flashing?"

"That is... that's the, you know, the... indicates the power!"

"It's on isn't it? I knew it! Oh God how embarrassing!"

"Sandy... just relax and concentrate, it's just a game, it's not for real. Let me put some music on to help you, OK?"

Danny enters the scene with the confidence of the Cecil De Mille of home videos. He's also around thirty-five, slightly balding, with a moustache, a type more suitable for mortgage deals than film stardom. He goes to the stereo system and with the consummate skill of the tech wizard puts a CD on. The abused Ravel's Bolero is played. The poor woman is now trying a pathetic striptease.

The frock is so tight that her movements get more and more clumsy, especially as she tries to follow the music. With a final effort the dress comes off. She's now wearing a black laced body, net stockings with relative suspenders. The result is more grotesque than sexy. She suddenly bursts into tears.

"I can't, I can't! I feel so ugly!"

"No! No! That was perfect! Carry on!"

"I can't go on, you try! And stop this music, is driving me crazy" She is almost hysterical.

Danny enters the scene again. He goes to the CD player. Music stops.

He now sits on the bed near Sandy. She's not a pretty sight: the mascara is running down her cheeks.

"C'mon it's nothing dirty, they would probably give it a PG certificate if screened."

"What's PG?"

"You know PG is when the good guy gets the girl, 15 when the bad guy gets the girl and 18 when everyone gets her!"

"So you get the girl then!" Sandy is laughing.

"I love you Sandy. I'm mad about you, you know that. I was just trying to do something for you!"

"For me? For me? I'm happy as I am! I don't need to watch dirty magazines or filthy videos to get aroused! Speak for yourself! This was your idea for your use or for God knows what!"

"What do you mean?"

"You and your friends making fun of me."

"You're nuts! You know it's not true, well yes we've joked and played the fool a few times but, they've nothing to do with this, this is for us, just you and me. (softly) C'mon pet... you know I can't resist you."

He's kissing her with passion on the shoulder. She's enjoying it.

"Oh Danny, my little stallion."

"Oh Sandy."

"Oh Danny."

They roll over the bed, entangled. We see Sandy reaching a switch on the bedhead and the light goes off. We hear their moaning and giggles in the dark.

Sandy is quite loud: "That's nice, yes, yes, run your fingers through my hair... oh that's so nice, but gently, do it gently."

"What are you doing? Are you taking off my trousers? First you are up here kissing my neck and then you're down at my feet, Sandy... Sandy?"

"Yes?"

"Why did you switch the light off?"

"Uhmm!"

"Sandy, wait!"

"Umpfh..."

"Not so hard, it hurts... Sandy! Gentle... ouch!"

The light is switched on again. Sandy is sitting on the bed, back to camera, expertly sucking Danny's right big toe. Danny is lying on his back holding the light switch in one hand, looking down at Sandy.

"Sandy! I'm asking you why you've switched off the light."

"I don't know it seemed-"

"Sandy! Now I have to run the tape backwards and we have to start all over again."

Sandy is gobsmacked: "I wasn't playing, I was really getting-"

"I know, and that's why I wanted to capture it on tape."

"That's typical of you, you're so vain. I've watched you when we have one of my girlfriends around and you look like you had peacock feathers sticking out your ass!"

"Sandy! You've never mentioned this before!"

"Well I do now and I'm sick of your sex games."

"If it wasn't for me you would still be convinced that babies come out of the belly button."

"Look who's talking: who was it the first time we got intimate, kept pushing his thingie into my belly button and gave me a sore one?"

"Oooh, the expert! Because you thought that babies came out of your stomach you didn't let me come in your belly button!"

They're now both sitting on the bed, in total silence.

"You don't even know what my... erogenous (she can't pronounce it properly) zones are."

"Your what?"

"Exactly."

"Listen, what I know is that when we make it I always give you an orgasm."

"What a word! You like that but you don't even know what it is! Coming from your mouth it sounds like some kind of disease! I can hear the news: 'Scientist dies in terrible pain after injecting himself by mistake with lethal dose of orgasm!' You men don't have the foggiest idea of how we women feel!"

Danny is astonished: "You've never talked like that, is it you Sandy? Is it still you in there?"

He taps his knuckles on her head.

"Don't patronise me Danny."

"I don't. I adore you honey."

"Don't honey me, it makes me diabetic."

Danny looks very sad. Sandy after a moment of silence puts her right arm around his shoulders.

She speaks to him softly: "I'm sorry, I didn't mean it Danny, really."

"It didn't sound like you, you've never behaved like that..

"It's that bloody thing (points to the camera) staring at us. I can't relax. It makes me nervous."

"OK, maybe it was a naff idea, but I thought it might have been exciting watching it some other time."

"I think those kinds of things look very sad in the end they just don't seem natural, they make you feel as if you're peeping on someone."

"But it would be just us on the screen."

"So, what's the difference? And can you imagine if someone manages to get hold of it by mistake?"

"Like who?"

"Well, Rose for instance; last time she came to do the cleaning she took home the tape of my sister's wedding by mistake thinking it was the video she rented."

"What does she rent videos for? She only likes Soaps."

"Danny you know that her son works at a TV station and he always asks her to rent videos to watch on the night shift, to kill time."

 "Oh shit!"

"What?"

"A trouser button is missing, you little tiger."

"Leave your trousers near the tapes, I'll tell Rose to fix it when she comes tomorrow."

Fade to black, the end credits roll in.

7. SHOOTING SCHEDULE

I have quite a few friends in the military scattered in different parts of the world and some of the stories that they tell me can be quite interesting. One in particular stayed with me for a while, it was about this guy who kept making these confessions to tape in case he would end up killed in action. One day his friends decided to play some while he wasn't there and they are still laughing about them, at the same time he got dismissed from the Army because his superiors truly realised how mentally sick he was.

I always wondered what could have been in those tapes.

Caption appears on black screen:
DEATH IS AN INHERITED DISEASE

The screen is then filled by a khaki mimetic pattern. It's a soldier in a combat suit moving away from the camera; we can see that we are in the desert, near a tent and some campfire nearby. Everything is khaki coloured, even the sand, only the soldier's face stands out. He's obviously a mercenary. No insignia on his combat suit. There are lots of scars on his face devoured by acne in a very troubled youth. He must be in his late thirties. He's the classic tough-son-of-a- bitch. He's sitting on an ammunitions box. His voice is testosterone deep and quite scary.

"Hi buddy, remember me? It has been some time, huh? Yes it's me, Johnny! How are things, brown-nose? Still kissing asses at the Academy? By now you're probably some high rank big shot, huh? (he laughs saluting) You'll always be a rookie for me, you damned fool. I couldn't believe you fell for that anorexic brunette, you probably married her by now. I guess. Yo man, let's cut the crap; I'm sending you this because... because... fuck! Because you're the only one I know who can make some sense out of what I gotta do. Do you ever wonder how you're going to die? I do, because I don't want to embarrass my friends. Death is a very personal thing: you must not wait 'til some son of a bitch steals your death: you must decide on it yourself. And that's what I'm going to do. And since you're my only friend left, you should be present, so you won't be embarrassed when they tell you."

He takes out his gun. Holds it in front of his eyes, as if seeing it for the first time.

"I cannot stand people in this business talking to their weapons as if the metal could answer or as if they were sexy things. It's crap! There was this guy, very big guy, from Holland I think, we all called him Siegfried, because he was the Aryan prototype, well, this guy was so much in love with his machine gun that he used to shove the barrel up his ass and masturbate! You won't believe it but one night it fired because the asshole didn't unload it. What a hell of a one-bang-thank-you-maaam'!"

He starts laughing.

"Ah Jesus, so funny! How should I address you now, Captain? Major? You know that they kicked me out of the army a few days before I was going to make it to Captain? Not bad huh? And you know why? Because I was accused of rape. Of rape! What fuckin' rape? She was all hot and asking for it and you call that rape? She enjoyed every minute of it the whore! She deserved it. When I finished she was a hole on two legs! I couldn't believe she had the heart to report it! That's water under the bridge anyway, I've changed, you see (he looks around). I don't drink, I don't smoke, I even pray to the Lord, not bad huh? So I think you'll probably want to know why I chose you, I'll tell you why: I'm tired. I'm tired of killing. I'm tired of being with people with the brain the size of a 12 mm gauge. I'm sick to the bloody teeth of all this. Yeah it's good money but there must be something more than that, like values, that's what a man needs."

He looks around nervously, worried that someone can hear him. He lowers his voice.

"Shit, I sound like one of those fuckin' preachers on the telly."

He stops; plays with his boot on the sand.

"Six months ago I get this job, doesn't matter where, some shitty place in East Africa, there was this local war going on and I was asked to instruct these zombies to shoot at targets, instead of blowing their feet away before aiming. So I get there, I think I've seen a lot but man, it's really, a joke! So the second day somehow some of them have captured a bunch of rebels, most of them wounded, so the 'officer' (sarcastic) in charge asks me what to do with them and I tell him to dispose of them, you know, so this fat asshole puts all the prisoners in line, takes his gun out and starts shooting them one by one, in the stomach. Now most of these bastards were just skin and bone, they didn't even feel the bullet going through and they kept standing still, bleeding and staring at him. So he comes back to me and says: 'They don't die.' So I calmly replied to him: 'You have to shoot them in the head', so the stupid fucker goes back to the line of bones, with a big grin on his shitty face, aims at the nearest one and shoots him in the head. Well you can imagine the head blew up like a watermelon and right on the officer's face. He had brains all over himself and he walks back to me again and shouts out of his mind 'It's not funny!' So you see..."

He leans towards the camera a bit more.

"That's what I have to put up with these days! It's the same shit everywhere. A week ago I'm training this middle-east terrorist and for no reason he takes out his knife and holds it to my throat and barks: 'Are you afraid to die, big man?' So I said: 'Not at all: on the contrary, it would be a big relief! Then I wouldn't have to train to be an asshole like you.' Next he was staring Allah in the eyeballs, looking for his promised virgins. You know I think we struggle in this game for nothing; it's too big man. It's like being a flea on the ass of an elephant. You're on your own as a man. I was sitting in a pigsty of a bar in Thailand, late at night, drinking on my own, and this old prostitute sat next to me and said: 'Look at you soldier, you have more in common with any of the men in this place than with the woman you'll ever be closest to in your life.' Gee, scary shit! The old bitch was right, but everything is changing; no more camaraderie, no proper man's talking anymore; the world is full of big-mouthed small dicked brats. I can field-strip a MAG in eight seconds sharp or fire a MG 42, you know, the Hitler's zipper, with one arm, all 1,200 rounds in one go! Doesn't that mean anything? What can today's toy soldiers do? Huh? You tell me! Frighten the hell out of some empty bottles fifty yards away? These sissies are queering the field, I tell you."

There is a moment of silence. He takes the gun and put it in his mouth. After a few terrible seconds he takes it away with a big grin.

"I'm not afraid of pulling the trigger; death is what makes life an event. Killing yourself is an act of supreme courage. Look at the Japanese for instance, small dicks but big hearts, they fear nothing but getting into a sauna with me! (He laughs loudly) But man! What warriors they make! Yeah, I'm not afraid of death. I've zipped up too many body bags. For me it's not a question of 'is there life after death' but 'is there life before death.' And don't think I've turned into some kind of philosopher; my heart is too close to my belly to understand what the head has to say. But still I can't stop thinking about where we all go. I wonder sometimes if one can come back from places where one has never been. I read a lot you know. There's not much action anymore, what we have to kill mostly is time nowadays, so I read. It's good for you: I keep reading stuff like 'what you don't know won't hurt you' or 'the less you know the better'. Crap like 'ignorance is bliss' well, good luck in this rotten world pal, I did-n't get where I'm now asking myself what do I think of life, but what life thinks of me!"

He pauses, breathing deeply.

"That's what it's all about. And I tell you soldiers of fortune are an endangered species, a dying breed like the cowboys. It's a shame because we take great care in what we do, it's a mission! I have read that Mother-fuckin'-Theresa once said: 'We can do no great things, only small things with great love!' That's exactly the point: I bet if she had a willy between her balls she would have been one of us."

Johnny stops for a while, almost catatonic, eyes star-ing into nothing, reflecting the vacuum in his brain.

"I love my job: it's like sex and pizza: even when it's bad it's still quite good. Man! I want to shoot so bad I can taste it. But no! Now everything has to be "politically correct" (sarcastic) and bullshit like that. You know why I have really stopped smoking? Because every time I used to put a fag in my lips there was some polite dickhead saying: 'Sorry sir, but you can't smoke in here' (mocking way) I couldn't keep smashing everyone's nose for that! It was much easier just to quit smoking, too many big-nosed polite faggots around! So I have had enough, this is the last job I'm doing; we've never fired, not even once! And there's no way anyone can understand how I feel, if I have to explain they won't understand. But I'm sure you will, we're the same, whether you admit it or not."

A man's voice is heard, together with the laughing and cheering of other soldiers in the background.

"Hey Johnny! Mama San has some new girls, yummy stuff, you comin'?"

Johnny's answers briskly.

"Not now!"

"C'mon man! Are you turning into some fuckin' monk or something?"

"NOT NOW I SAID!"

"OK, OK, cool down!"

The voices fade in the distance followed by silence. Johnny he's now loading his gun. We hear the sinister sound of the chamber welcoming the bullet. He pulls the hammer.

"This baby is the only reliable relationship I've never had, she'd never let me down. Maybe she really has a soul, a blue steel one (looks at it closer), not a spot of rust, unlike me, I'm the one who's rusting. I talk too much, and you know what? I don't think my schedule is completed yet, not yet, there's so much to do."

He aims the gun towards the camera and fires at it. As the lens shutters and the screen goes black we hear his last words before the tape stops completely:

"Mama San, he said."

Fade to black, the end credits roll in.

8. ROADKILL

Traditionally I come from a film animation background, anything from stop motion to cells under a rostrum camera; therefore I always had a soft spot for it.

Animators are a funny breed and I could not resist when a friend who is a CGI artist, a modern day computer animator, asked me if I could write him a short script in the style of Pixar, the people behind 'Toy Story' and 'Finding Nemo'. So this is it, I don't know if it will ever be seen on a screen one day, but probably still makes a good bedtime story for kids.

Fade in.

We see one, just one, apple, against a beautiful sky.

This is no ordinary apple, this is a real treat, the most delicious mouth watering taste buds pleaser around.

As we move away we can see that it is also the only apple left on the tree.

As we observe it from different angles, a drop of morning dew slowly moves down the perfect shape, it really could be the start of an expensive TV juice ad.

We follow the drop as it complies with the laws of gravity and falls towards earth.

The drop lands on the tiniest cutest nose you can imagine.

The nose belongs to a hedgehog standing under the tree looking up in a stare at the forbidden fruit.

The drop makes him sneeze but he quickly regains his posture not to lose sight of the precious fruit.

As we move around we can see the sharp points of his spiky armour ready to welcome such an appetizing beauty.

A sudden gentle gut of wind shakes the branch holding our beautiful apple.

Our little spiky hero follows with trepidation the swinging movements of the branch holding the apple, we can hear the nervous panting as he adjusts his position to make sure the apple will land right on his body.

More adjustments.

A quick check.

Left. Right.

Back! Back!

Hooonk!

The blasting sound of a truck's horn makes him jolt.

We move away even farther away to discover that he is near a busy road, a highway in fact.

We see the truck speeding past, enormous, mean.

The air movement caused by the speeding mammoth shakes the tree.

In slow motion the branch swivels back and forth, in teasing fashion, and with a sudden adjustment the apple breaks loose.

A series of quick editing cuts show our hedgehog desperately trying to reach the perfect position to catch the apple on his back. The precious fruit almost lands on him but suddenly is deviated by a large mushroom and then bounces back onto the tree's trunk, rolling viciously onto a root, deflected by a large leaf, finally somersaulting into the middle of the highway.

Heavy traffic appears from nowhere; trucks cars, motorbikes, a caravan, even an ambulance. The world is in motion, at the worst ever time.

We see our little hedgehog frozen aghast as he follows the apple slowly rolling onto the opposite end of the road. Every second all sorts of wheels, from huge trucks to a tiny Lambretta closely shave the apple.

The hedgehog's expression says it all.

But there's a God! Miraculously the apple gently stops in the ditch side lining the highway, not a scratch, untouched.

We can hear the long sigh of the hedgehog relieving his soul tearing tension.

Our spiky hero is now observing more traffic speeding past, this is an impossible mission.

Time goes by and in a time lapse sequence we see the hedgehog looking at the apple, then the motorway busy with traffic.

The sun sets peacefully and the traffic is now calming, headlamps piercing the darkness.

We see the apple resting in the ditch, every headlight going past is flashing the gorgeous fruit, a visual torture for our little hero.

In his eyes, a little tear, then we hear the loud swallowing of saliva as he looks at the apple.

More time goes past, the road sees less and less traffic.

Our hedgehog keeps looking right, then left, examining the empty road in almost total darkness except for a feeble moonlight, the tarmac looking incredibly reassuring.

He tries a trembling step, quietly and stealthily, not a mechanical sound can be heard from anywhere, just the reassuring noise of crickets in the stillness of the night.

Our hero is reassured and tries more decisive steps as he keeps looking in both directions.

A bird's eye view of our hedgehog, in the middle of the road; he looks vulnerable.

We can then see as he sees, looking in the distance, the white middle line disappearing into the darkness.

His eyes suddenly are widening with fear, two yellow spots growing in size from far, approaching fast.

A car?

 A van?

A truck?

Wooosh.

Just an owl, flying past.

Nearly dead with fear we see the hedgehog as he resumes his walk recovering from a serious scare.

As he reaches the other end, a sudden resurgence of traffic comes suddenly from nowhere, several trucks speeding past, and horn blown at deafening levels.

Our hedgehog is white with fear but slowly gets back to his usual self.

The apple, a triumph of appetizing beauty, in all its glory is now so close. He tries to roll onto the apple, to pierce it with his sharp back.

We can hear lots of huffing and puffing, with some really funny positions trying to impale the apple.

Frustrated he finally decides to push it back onto the road, empty while the traffic has now disappeared.

Our hero is now negotiating the road again, his precious item in front of his nose, and he is moving gently, with an easy rolling motion.

He then reaches the middle of the road, sweat pouring from his spiky forehead.

A pause is necessary in order to recover.

He looks around, hearing a distant thunder.

A storm?

A twister?

Wroomm…

It's a truck approaching, ominous, unstoppable, faster, closer.

Our hero looks in the opposite direction, there is also a car approaching. It's a family car with parents, kids and a dog, a little terrier.

A scream comes loud from the car as the children have spotted the hedgehog in the middle of the road and so has the little terrier, now jumping furiously onto the dashboard, barking mad.

The father is trying to keep the car under control.

Our hedgehog is watching all this, on one side the family car swerving dangerously while opposite the truck is approaching, horn blaring demanding its way.

The truck finally loses control narrowly missing the incoming car with screaming children, terrified parents and barking mad dog.

The screaming passengers and the frothy at the mouth terrier are disappearing in the distance, but the truck is now skidding onto the road on his side, sparks vomiting everywhere.

Our hedgehog is staring at his apple, well... what is left of it, because the family car has squashed to a pulp the beautiful fruit. Shock, horror and a sense of doom flashing in our hedgehog's expression as he stares at the truck, he seems accepting his impending fate.

The truck comes to a stop inches away from the frozen hedgehog in a volcano of sparks and burnt rubber smoke, as its load comes loose.

A ton of apples, fresh, fruity, beautiful, gorgeous fruits submerge our little hero.

As the load plummets everything falls silent, the only noise coming from the wheels still spinning and crushed metal coming to rest.

We admire the mountain of apples glinting in the morning rising sun.

Nothing moves but then a few apples start falling from a corner of the pile as our little hero emerges from under the mountain, his back loaded with juicy fruit.

He walks triumphantly in the rising sun, enjoying the dew in the field.

We move away, high up, watching the vast field cut slowly by our little rubble of apples moving in the grass.

We move higher even further to reveal that the field is in fact an airfield with a well maintained grass landing strip.

A small plane is just approaching to land, his landing gear lining up perfectly with a slow moving rubble of apples in the grass.

Fade to black, the end credits roll in.

About the Author

Francesco Pagot was born near Venice, Italy not California, and was educated in the classics. His celluloid addiction brings him to Milan, where he works all sorts to support his habit. In 1989 he moved to London, eventually establishing himself as a cinematographer.

After winning a Creative Review writing competition he intensified his efforts, writing screenplays that have won awards, produced and sold. He lives in London.

www.ingramcontent.com/pod-product-compliance
Lightning Source LLC
Chambersburg PA
CBHW030637130626
46552CB00002B/893